Ravenscourt
B·O·O·K·S

KING MIDAS
and the
GOLDEN TOUCH

**A Greek Myth
Retold by
Carole H. Gerber**

**Illustrated by
Pat Lucas-Morris**

Columbus, OH • Chicago, IL • Redmond, WA

The **McGraw·Hill** Companies

SRAonline.com

 **SRA**

Send all inquiries to:
SRA/McGraw-Hill
8787 Orion Place
Columbus, OH 43240-4027

Printed in the United States of America.

ISBN 0-07-601586-6

2 3 4 5 6 7 8 9 MAL 08 07 06 05 04

CHAPTER 1

The Two Loves of King Midas

Long ago in a place far away, a baby boy was born. His name was Midas. One day while Midas was taking a nap, ants put grains of wheat on his lips.

His family was sure it was a sign. They asked an oracle—a man who can see the future. The oracle said that one day Midas would be rich and powerful.

The oracle was right. Midas became king of a land called Phrygia.

He was rich, and he was powerful. But Midas was also foolish.

The people of Phrygia were not rich, but King Midas lived in a big palace.

The people had little food to eat, but the king ate big meals.

The people had plain hats, but the king had a golden crown.

The people didn't have many coins, but the king had a room full of them. Yet, Midas was not happy. He wanted more.

"I need more gold!" he fretted. "I must find a way to get more." Midas liked to look at his gold coins. He liked to touch them and count them.

*"I like the sound gold coins make when I stack them," he said. "It is music to my ears!"

Midas loved only one thing as much as gold, and that was his daughter. Because no one wrote down her name, we will call her Kali, which means "rosebud." Midas fretted over Kali too.

"When I am gone, I must leave my child lots of gold," he said. "I need more gold now, so Kali can have more gold later."

Midas wished for gold in everything he saw. "If only that sunset were gold," he said, "I would get the rays* of the sun, and I would keep them for my daughter."

One day Midas and Kali were walking in their rose garden. At one time, Midas loved his roses almost as much as he loved Kali.

Kali stopped to smell the flowers. The king pulled her along.

"Slow down, Father!" she said. "You once liked smelling the roses."

"I would like them more if they were gold," he snapped.

CHAPTER 2

King Midas Makes a Wish

Kali felt sad. She hung her head. Then she saw an old man. He was asleep in the roses.

"Look, Father!" she said.

Midas tapped the man with his foot. "Who are you?" he asked. The man sat up and rubbed his eyes.

"I am Silenus," he said. "I became very tired and stopped to rest. I am on my way to see my old student. He is the Greek god Dionysus. I thought I knew the way there, but I am lost," said Silenus.

*King Midas was happy. He liked the god Dionysus. "You must be a very wise man," Midas said. "Come inside my house. We will give you something to eat. You can stay with us."

The king helped Silenus to his feet. King Midas and Kali took Silenus inside and fed him. Then they tucked him into bed. Midas said Silenus could stay as long as he liked.

Silenus was a good guest. He sang songs and told tales. He entertained the king and his daughter for ten days.

Then Silenus said he had to go. He was rested, and so* he set off to see Dionysus. Midas sent someone with Silenus to be sure he got there safely.

Dionysus was glad to hear that Midas had been kind to his old teacher Silenus.

Dionysus went to see King Midas. Then Dionysus told Midas he would grant him one wish.

"I will grant you any wish," Dionysus said. "Please think carefully about it."

King Midas felt very lucky. "There is no need to wait," he said. "I already know what I want. I want everything I touch to turn to gold."

Dionysus seemed upset. "Are you sure?" he asked. "Do you want to think about this some more?"

"No," said Midas. "I do not need to think about it. Please grant this wish. I want to be the richest king in the land."

Dionysus shook his head. Then he waved his hand.

"I have granted your wish," he said. "You now have the golden touch. Midas, you were kind to Silenus, but you are a foolish man."

—CHAPTER 3—

How Good Is the Golden Touch?

Midas was very happy. He did not hear Dionysus's warning. He thanked Dionysus and waved to him as he left.

Then Midas jumped up and down. He was so happy he started to shout. He could not wait to try the golden touch.

"Go slowly," he said to himself. "Start with little things."

He picked up a small stone. It turned to gold. He picked up a bigger stone. It also turned to gold.

*Midas's heart beat faster. "It's true!" he shouted. "It works! I have the golden touch.

"Oh, thank you, great Dionysus! Thank you! Thank you! I am the luckiest man in the land. And soon I will be the richest."

Midas hummed as he put one hundred stones in neat stacks.

"I'll pick these up later," he said. "Now I will try my touch on bigger things."

He opened the door to go inside. The door turned to gold! Midas smiled from ear to ear.

"Oh, my!" he shouted. "Much better than the old door."

Midas walked all over the palace*
and touched every door. Each one
turned to gold.

He walked into his bedroom and
picked up his robe. More gold!

Midas touched his dresser and his
drinking cup. Gold! Gold! He touched
his bed frame and blankets. Soon his
bedroom shone with gold.

Midas grinned. "Soon I will have a
golden palace," he said. "There will be
no other like it."

That gave Midas another idea. He
went outside and ran around the
palace. He touched every wall. The
wood and stone turned to gold.

"I have done some lovely work," he said. "But now I am tired. I need to rest awhile before dinner."

Midas touched a stone bench. It turned to gold. That made him smile. Then he sat down to enjoy his golden palace.

—CHAPTER 4—

How Bad Is the Golden Touch?

Midas rested for a short while. Then he started feeling hungry. "Time to eat," he said happily.

He could not wait to turn his knife, plate, and cup into gold. He skipped into the dining room. His meal was ready for him.

Midas pulled out his chair. It turned to gold. He grinned. Then he picked up his knife. Gold! He touched his plate. Gold! He picked up his cup. Gold!

He took a drink. But wait! He couldn't drink the water. It had turned to gold.

Midas didn't understand. He shook his head.

Carefully he cut his meat. Slowly he put the meat to his lips. When he bit into it, the meat turned to gold. "Maybe I can eat if someone else feeds me," said Midas.

He called for his cook. He asked for a new plate of food. He demanded a new cup of water. Then he ordered a servant to feed him.

The servant picked up a piece of meat. It did not turn to gold. Midas was thankful. He opened his mouth.

As soon as the meat touched his mouth, it turned to gold. The servant screamed.

*"Water!" Midas ordered. "Please give me a drink of water."

The woman picked up the cup. Her hands shook as she lifted it. As soon as the water touched the king's lips, it turned to gold.

The servant dropped the cup. "Don't touch me!" she yelled at Midas. Then she ran out of the room.

Midas picked up the napkin that lay next to his plate. It turned to gold. Midas threw the napkin to the floor. It landed with a thud.

Midas got up. "Maybe a walk in my rose garden will take my mind off food," he said.*

CHAPTER 5

King Midas Learns a Lesson

Midas walked slowly through the palace. The golden doors did not cheer him. He couldn't stop thinking about food. "How will I fix this?" he asked himself. "I must find a way to eat."

His stomach growled. "Stop it," he ordered. His stomach did not stop. It growled again and again.

Midas sat on his gold bench and looked at his garden. The wind carried the smell of roses to his nose.

Midas said, "The smell of my roses always cheers me."

*He got up and bent over a rose. He sniffed the flower. It turned to gold. He bent and touched another rose with his nose. Gold!

"It's clear to me now," he said. "The golden touch is not just in my fingers. Making a garden of gold will help me forget my hunger," he said.

Midas walked in the garden, touching each rose. There were many roses. It took him a long time. But turning the roses to gold made him feel good. He even forgot about his hunger.

Then Midas noted something bad. He could not smell the roses.* There were only stiff, golden roses.

"I will miss smelling the roses," he said sadly. "Maybe I should have left some of the roses untouched."

Suddenly his daughter came up behind him. "Father!" Kali cried. "What have you done to our garden?"

He turned quickly to tell her not to touch him. It was too late! She tugged his arm.

His little girl had turned to gold. Two golden tears lay on each cheek. She had a golden frown on her face. Kali had turned from his dear child into a golden statue.

Midas fell to the ground. "I hate this," he sobbed. "I must rid myself of the golden touch."

—CHAPTER 6—

Good-bye to the Golden Touch

All night Midas lay crying beside the statue. The next morning he picked up his pen to write to Dionysus. It turned to gold. Midas was very unhappy.

He wrote slowly. He was careful not to touch the paper.

"Dionysus, I have been a foolish man," he wrote. "The golden touch is not good. My dear daughter is a statue. I will die because I cannot eat. I am begging you. Please free me from the golden touch." A servant folded the note and took it to Dionysus.

*Dionysus came quickly. "Are you sure you want to give up the golden touch?" he asked. "What have you learned?"

"I am wiser now," Midas cried. "I would not trade a corner of my daughter's smile for all the gold in the land.

"I would not trade a crust of bread for a sea of gold," he said. "I would not trade a drink of water for a golden sky. Simple things are far better than palaces made of gold."

Dionysus smiled. "So you wish to rid yourself of the golden touch?" he asked.

"Yes! Yes! Yes!" cried Midas. "Please* take it away from me!"

"Take a pitcher, and go to the river that runs past your garden," Dionysus said. "Jump into the river. Fill the pitcher with water. Then put the water on everything you wish had not turned to gold."

Midas grabbed a gold pitcher. He ran to the river. As soon as he jumped in, the pitcher turned back into clay. He shouted with joy. He filled the pitcher with water.

Midas ran to Kali. He put water on her golden face. She turned back into a little girl. He kissed and hugged her.

Then he ran around the garden and the palace. He put water on everything gold.

27

All day Midas refilled the pitcher with water from the river. All day he turned things back from gold. He stopped only to eat and drink. By nightfall, all the gold was gone. Only the brown sand beside the river remained gold.